THE USBORNE SOCC

ATTACKING

Richard Dungworth
Designed by Neil Francis

Illustrations by Bob Bond • Photographs by Chris Cole
Edited by Gill Harvey • Managing designer: Stephen Wright
Managing editor: Felicity Brooks
Consultant: John Shiels,
Bobby Charlton International Soccer Schools Ltd.

Special thanks to players Kevin Better, Botlme Bolot-ete, Ben Dale, Deps Gabonamong,
Hardiker, David Hughes, Michael Jones, Otlaadisa Mohambi, Leanne Prince, Daniel
Savastano, John Tabas, Joe Vain, and to their coaches, Bryn Cooper and Alex Black

Library photographs: Allsport UK • Cover photograph: Empics
Soccer boots courtesy of Reebok UK

DTP by John Russell

CONTENTS

INTO ATTACK

To win a soccer match, you need to score goals – and to score goals, you need to attack. Whenever your team has the ball, you and your team-mates should be looking for ways to attack your opponents' goal, set up a chance to shoot, and score. This book looks at the individual and team skills you will need to do this successfully.

WHAT MAKES A GOOD ATTACKER?

Intelligence
An attacker's top priority is to spot any defensive weaknesses, and make intelligent choices to exploit them.

Fitness and confidence
A player with stamina, pace and a real belief in himself can put the defence under constant pressure.

Control
To make sure his team keeps possession in an attack, a player needs to move confidently with the ball, and pass accurately.

Team spirit
Solo skills alone won't win matches. A good attacker is always thinking of how he can work well with his team-mates.

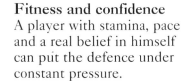

Cunning
A predictable attack is easy to defend against. An attacker must disguise his intentions, and vary his approach.

Determination
The 'will to win' is crucial for good attacking play. The best attackers play fairly, but are very competitive.

FIT FOR ATTACK

Professional soccer players train regularly so that they have the skills and fitness they need to play well throughout the 90 minutes of a match. They combine this with a healthy diet, as both diet and exercise are important for staying fit.

Here, the players in blue tracksuits are using long track runs in training to build up their stamina.

The red players are using special sprinting routines, called 'shuttle runs', to improve their pace.

STAGES OF ATTACK

An attack begins when your team wins possession of the ball. This book looks at the stages of attack which follow.

1. You need to move the ball upfield into the 'attacking third' (the final third of the pitch). Pages 4-13 cover this first stage, known as the 'build-up'.

The final pass is often known as the 'assist'.

2. For your team to score, you need to get the ball to a player who is in a good position to shoot. Pages 14-21 look at the skills involved in this second stage of an attack.

3. The picture below shows the final stage of attack – the shot at goal, or 'finish'. Pages 22-27 cover shooting techniques and tactics.

'SMALL-SIDED' TEAM PRACTICE

The skills in this book can help you and your team-mates strengthen your attacking play, but only if you back them up with regular team practice.

If you have an odd number of players, one can be the referee.

Mark out a short, wide pitch, so that most of the action is around the goalmouth areas.

Use 'small-sided' games, with two teams of five or more players, to practise the attacking techniques and tactics described in this book.

RUNNING OFF THE BALL

Each player has only a few minutes of possession during the course of a match. You spend the rest of the time playing without, or 'off' the ball. Success in attack therefore depends on how good you and your team-mates are at running off the ball to find good positions on the pitch.

FINDING SPACE IN A GOOD POSITION

When your team is attacking, try to move into a position on the pitch where you can receive a pass, and where you will pose a threat to the other team's defence once you have the ball.

Try to find space upfield, so that by receiving a pass you move play towards goal.

If your team-mate can't pass straight upfield, move so he can reach you with an angled pass.

LOSING YOUR MARKER

As you move off the ball, one of your opponents will try to stay close to you to prevent you from receiving the ball. He is your 'marker'. Finding a good position is pointless if he is close enough to intercept a pass, so use a sudden change of direction to get away from him.

Draw your marker away from the area you want to run into, by moving off in the opposite direction first.

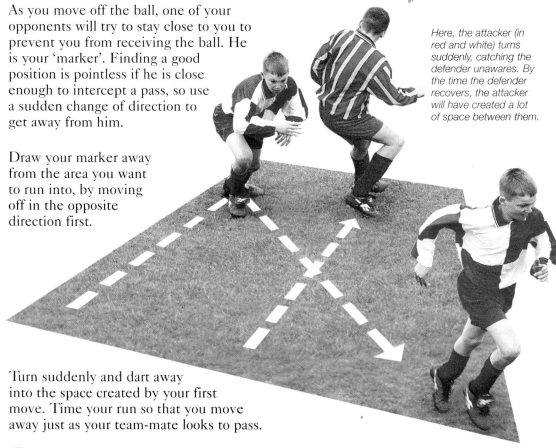

Here, the attacker (in red and white) turns suddenly, catching the defender unawares. By the time the defender recovers, the attacker will have created a lot of space between them.

Turn suddenly and dart away into the space created by your first move. Time your run so that you move away just as your team-mate looks to pass.

'PASS AND RUN' PLAY

Here, this defender begins to follow the pass.

If you've just passed the ball, don't stop and relax. Your marker will often follow your pass, giving you an immediate chance to dart away from him.

Free of his marker, the attacker who passed can move into space.

Move into space as soon as you've released the ball. This 'pass and run' play, also known as 'give and go' play, is one key to successful attack.

DIAGONAL RUNS

Even if you don't receive the ball yourself, running off the ball can draw your marker away to create space for a team-mate. A diagonal run upfield is especially good for pulling defenders out of position.

Above, player A makes a diagonal run. His marker follows him, leaving space for B to collect the ball (below).

STAYING ONSIDE

You can't receive a pass if you are 'offside'. You are offside if you are nearer your opponent's goal-line than the ball when it is passed to you, unless two or more of your opponents are at least as close to their goal-line. You can't be offside in your own half of the pitch.

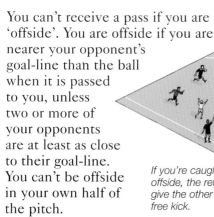

If you're caught offside, the referee will give the other team a free kick.

When you're running off the ball in attack, make sure you don't take up an offside position. You'll find out more about how to stay onside on page 14.

BASIC MOVES

To move play into the attacking third, you need to combine intelligent running off the ball with controlled, accurate passing. These pages introduce some simple passing moves that you can use to push play upfield past your opponents.

MAKING A BLINDSIDE RUN

One good way of finding space upfield is to make a run behind an opponent's back, outside his field of view. This is known as making a blindside run.

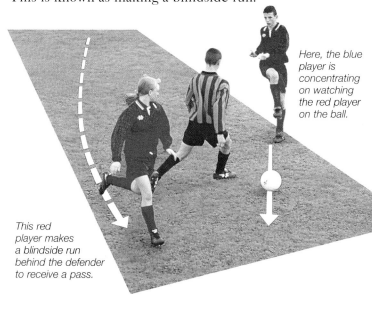

Here, the blue player is concentrating on watching the red player on the ball.

This red player makes a blindside run behind the defender to receive a pass.

Above, a blindside run forms the second part of a 'pass and run' attacking move. Player A passes to player B. As the yellow player moves in to challenge B, A makes a run around his blindside. Player B hits a return pass upfield into A's path.

BEATING BALL-WATCHERS

Try to catch defenders 'ball-watching'. This means paying too much attention to play elsewhere on the pitch, instead of to their own positions. Grab your chance to make a blindside run into a good position.

Here, the green player takes advantage of his marker's lapse of concentration, making a blindside run behind him.

OVERLAPPING

Doing an 'overlap run' means running past a team-mate on the ball and into space upfield, so that he can pass the ball back up to you. A simple overlap move, like the one shown here, is a particularly good way of pushing the attack upfield along one of the wings.

Here, player A passes to his team-mate and follows his pass, overlapping to receive a return ball.

WALL PASSES

A wall pass, or 'one-two', is a great way of getting past a player. To do this, dribble straight at your opponent. Just before he challenges you, send a sideways pass to a team-mate. Your opponent will turn to follow the play, giving you a chance to sprint past him. Your team-mate acts as the wall, knocking the ball back into your path.

★ Don't pass the ball too soon or your opponent will be able to drop back and block the move.

★ The wall player needs to move into position at the very last moment, so that he loses his marker.

★ Make sure both passes are fast enough to beat the defender, but not too difficult for the receiver to control.

WALL PASS GAME

Mark out an area 24 x 6m (80 x 20ft) and divide it into four equal 'zones'. Five attackers and four defenders take up starting positions as shown.

The player with the ball tries to take it from one end to the other. He can dribble past a defender, or use a wall pass. He scores a point for each zone he crosses.

Change around so that each player has a go at being the dribbler and a wall player.

Use sports markers, bags or sweaters to mark out the game area.

BUILDING AN ATTACK

Good attacking play needs team co-ordination and co-operation, as well as individual running and passing skills. To build an attack, you and your team-mates need to work together to make the most of the space available on the pitch, and to keep the defence guessing.

GIVING AN ATTACK WIDTH

If all your attacking players gather around the player on the ball, so that they are clustered together in one area of the pitch, your attack will be easy to defend against.

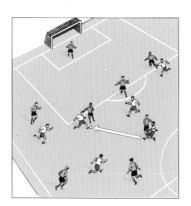

Spread out across the pitch, so that your opponents are forced to defend across its whole width. By passing across the pitch, you can quickly change the path of attack.

WING ATTACKS

Your opponents will try to protect the central area of their defensive third, in front of their goal. You can often push upfield into attack more easily by passing the ball to a team-mate on the wing, where there is more space.

Here, Steve McManaman (Liverpool) beats his opponent on the wing.

GIVING AN ATTACK DEPTH

If your players form a flat line across the pitch, they have few passing options, and very little chance of breaking past the defence. Try to stagger your players, so you can use diagonal passing up and downfield to give your attack depth and flexibility.

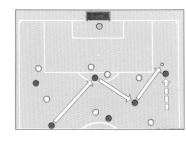

Below, the zigzag spacing of the blue attackers gives their attack depth.

Make sure you stay onside as you push upfield.

USING A CROSS-OVER MOVE

A cross-over move is when you and a team-mate run past each other to confuse your opponents.

A cross-over move can be played with or without the ball. To play one with the ball, dribble across the pitch towards a team-mate who is running in the opposite direction.

As your paths cross, flick the ball across into your team-mate's path. He can take advantage of the defenders' confusion, and the space behind them, to push upfield into attack.

Above, player A looks to pass. B drops back as though to receive the ball, taking his marker with him. Player C 'crosses over' with B, and runs past him to receive the pass from A.

A cross-over move like this is a great way to change the direction of attack suddenly.

As with a cross-over off the ball, the aim is to draw two defenders together to create space elsewhere on the pitch.

COMBINING SKILLS FOR TEAM ATTACK

This is an example of how a team can combine good positioning, intelligent runs off the ball and accurate passing to build an attack and create a chance to score. The move starts with player A on the ball, moving up from midfield.

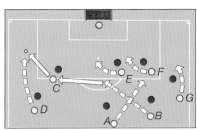

A and B use a cross-over move to switch the attack to C. Player D makes an overlapping run onto a pass from C. E and F draw their markers left.

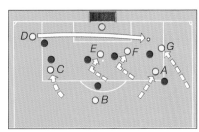

Player G runs into a good striking position, blindside of the defenders, to receive a long cross from D. The other players move up in support.

MOVING WITH THE BALL

If you have the ball and there is open space directly ahead, you can dribble upfield into attack rather than passing to a team-mate. For a solo run, you need good technique and confidence so that you can move quickly with the ball, changing pace and direction without losing control.

DRIBBLING TECHNIQUE

To keep the ball under close control as you move, use small, regular taps to push it gently forwards. Use different parts of your foot to steer the ball in the right direction. To improve your technique, mark out a slalom (a zigzag course) and dribble through it.

If you look down at the ball all the time as you dribble, you won't know where to direct your attack. If you and your team practise dribbling in a small area such as the centre circle, you can get used to looking up regularly to see where other players are.

Here, several players practise their dribbling within the centre circle.

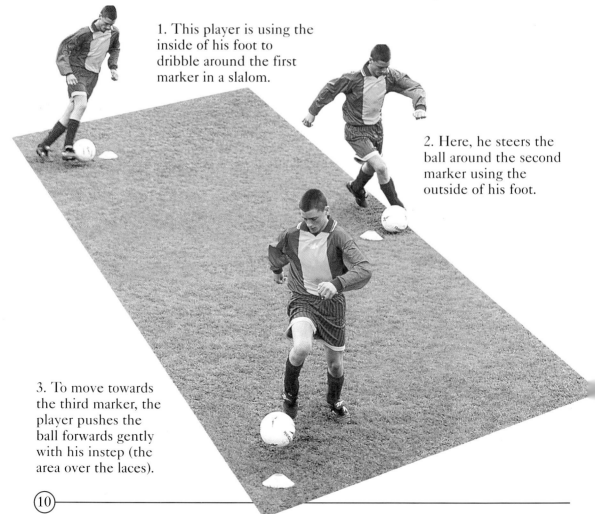

1. This player is using the inside of his foot to dribble around the first marker in a slalom.

2. Here, he steers the ball around the second marker using the outside of his foot.

3. To move towards the third marker, the player pushes the ball forwards gently with his instep (the area over the laces).

RUNNING WITH THE BALL

To attack at a fast pace, you need to move more quickly than a close dribbling technique allows. To run with the ball, use fewer touches, knocking it quite far ahead with each one, so that you can lengthen your stride and move faster.

Use the outside of your foot to knock the ball forward. Try to get a 'push and chase' rhythm that lets you run without breaking your stride.

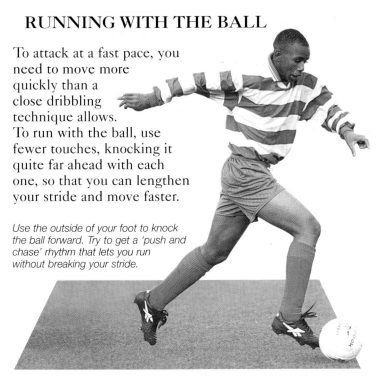

DRIBBLE AND SPRINT RELAY

This game will improve your skills on the ball. You need two teams, with a ball for each team. Lay out two identical slaloms, about 20m (66ft) apart. The teams start by forming two rows between the slaloms, facing in opposite directions.

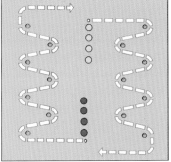

At the shout of 'Go!' the first player in each team starts a clockwise circuit with the ball, sprinting to the slalom on his right. He dribbles through the first slalom, and then sprints across towards the second.

SOLO ATTACK

1. If a defender closes in on you, but you can see that there is a lot of space upfield behind him, knock the ball firmly past him.

2. Quickly sprint past your opponent to collect the ball, before he can turn to follow you. This is known as 'taking on' a defender.

Once you're past the defender, push upfield into space.

If you win the ball when your opponents are on the attack, try to counter-attack before they can drop back to defend. You can use a solo run, at full stretch, to move upfield as quickly as possible.

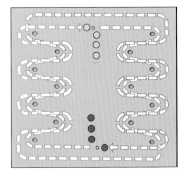

Next, he dribbles through the second slalom, and sprints back to his starting position. The next player takes the ball and begins his circuit. When one of the running players catches the other, his team wins.

POSITIONAL PLAY

To make the best use of the space on the pitch, professional teams play in a 'team formation'. This means that each of the ten outfield players takes up a particular position. These pages look at a typical '4-4-2' formation – four players in defence, four in midfield, and two in attack. You can also find out about how the roles of players in different positions contribute to the attack.

DEFENCE INTO ATTACK

The goalkeeper, centre backs and full backs are mainly responsible for defence. When they win the ball, though, they play an important attacking role by 'distributing' it upfield. This means making careful choices about where to pass the ball. Good distribution by defenders is vital if your team is to seize opportunities to counter-attack.

As a back, you can help to move the ball into attack by overlapping with midfield team-mates. Here, the red full back overlaps with the outside right.

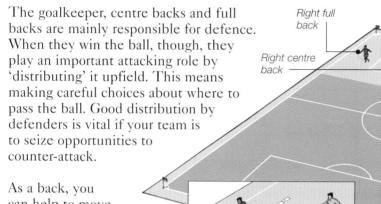

Right full back

Goalkeeper

Left full back

Right centre back

Left centre back

SKILLS IN MIDFIELD

Playing as a midfielder is all about moving the ball into a scoring position. You need to be able to create gaps in the defence by running off the ball, using intelligent and accurate passing to give an attack width and depth, and dribbling past defenders to threaten goal. You also need to shoot confidently whenever you get a chance.

The outside left and outside right, or 'wingers', need to perfect the skills of running with the ball and crossing it (see pages 16-19), so that they can attack along the wing.

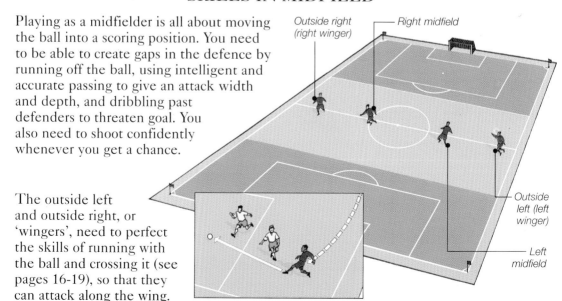

Outside right (right winger)

Right midfield

Outside left (left winger)

Left midfield

PLAYING CENTRE FORWARD

The main role of a centre forward, or 'striker', is to score goals. To be a successful striker you need excellent shooting and heading techniques so that you can score in a variety of situations. These may be when you receive a through ball (see page 14), a cross (see page 16), or when you are on the run. You also need to work on finding space, and staying onside (see page 14).

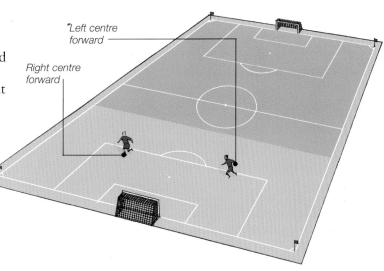

Left centre forward

Right centre forward

TARGET MAN

As centre forward, you play an important role as a 'target man'. This means that when one of your team-mates hits a long pass upfield to you, you are able to keep possession of the ball, 'holding it up' until your team-mates have moved up to support you.

Here, Gabriel Batistuta (Fiorentina) shields the ball, giving his team-mates time to move upfield.

TEAM TALK

Good positional play is only part of making the most of the pitch area. The other vital factor is good communication with your team-mates.

'Up the wing!'

If you're in a good position to receive a pass, call for the ball, or signal for it by raising your arm.

'Over!'

Shout if you think a team-mate should let the ball run on to you instead of playing it himself (see page 15).

'Man on!'

Warn your team-mate if you can see an opponent running in on his blindside to challenge him.

'And back!'

Talk your team-mates through a move. Here, the player calls for a return ball to complete a wall pass.

THE THROUGH BALL

Once your team has moved play upfield into the attacking third, you need to get the ball to a player who is in a good position to shoot. This is usually one of your strikers. A pass into space behind the defence for a team-mate to run onto and shoot is called a 'through ball'.

PLAYING A THROUGH BALL

A through ball requires good co-ordination between the passer and the receiver. If you pass the ball too late, the receiver will be caught offside. You also need to judge the weight of the pass. If it's too hard or too soft, a defender or the goalkeeper will be able to get to the ball first, and block your attack.

Here, the attacker kicks a diagonal through ball and the striker runs straight upfield to meet it.

Here, an attacker hits a pass straight upfield. His team-mate makes a diagonal run to collect the ball.

THE OFFSIDE TRAP

The other team may try to use a defensive tactic called the 'offside trap' to prevent your attack.

As an attacker prepares to play a through ball, the row of defenders rush forward together.

If they time the trap well, the defenders are likely to catch at least one of your players offside.

STAYING ONSIDE

If you're about to run onto a through ball, be alert in case the defence use the offside trap. Use these tactics to avoid being caught offside.

'Flatten' your run, and move across the pitch in line with the defenders until the moment your team-mate passes.

Make your run from midfield. Your team-mate then times his pass for when you draw level with the line of defenders.

If you play a through ball to yourself, you can't be offside. Knock the ball past defenders into space behind them, and sprint through to collect it (see page 11).

ONE TOUCH PLAY

When you receive the ball, you may see a chance to play it through to a team-mate. If so, try to use your first touch to play your pass, rather than taking time to control the ball. This gives your attack extra pace and surprise.

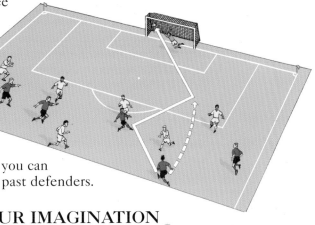

A wall pass (see page 7) on the edge of the penalty area, like the one shown here, is a great example of how you can use 'one touch play' in attack to break past defenders.

USING YOUR IMAGINATION

The more varied your passing, the harder it is for the other team to anticipate and block your attack. Look out for inventive ways to play the ball past the defence.

Your team-mate shouts 'Over!' to tell you to let the ball through.

For a 'dummy', or 'over', make as though to play the ball as it comes to you, but then let it run on to a team-mate beyond you.

If a defender has his legs wide apart as he jockeys, play a through ball between them. This is known as nutmegging him.

To play a through ball in an unexpected direction, use your heel to 'backheel' the ball to a team-mate behind you.

CROSSING TECHNIQUE

If you've built an attack down the wing, you need to get the ball back across the front of the opposition goal to give a team-mate the chance to shoot. Sending a long pass from the wing to a player in the centre is known as crossing the ball. More than half of all the goals scored in open play come from crosses.

TARGET AREAS

The idea of a cross is to move the ball from the wing, where it is difficult to shoot or score from, into the 'danger area' behind the defence and in front of the goal.

You can use different lengths of cross to create different attacking moves. The three main areas to aim for, shown below, are called the near post, mid-goal and far post areas.

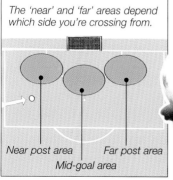

The 'near' and 'far' areas depend which side you're crossing from.

Near post area   Far post area
Mid-goal area

CROSSING TECHNIQUE

To hit a cross, you use the inside of your foot to strike through the lower half of the ball. Strike the ball slightly off-centre. This makes it spin, so that your cross swings into the target area.

Take a good backswing.

Get your non-kicking foot slightly behind and to the side of the ball.

Kick the lower half of the ball to make it rise.

Wrap your foot around the outside of the ball as you kick, to make it spin.

Swing your kicking leg across your body as you follow through.

GETTING IN YOUR CROSS

You need to be able to cross even if you are being jockeyed by an opponent.

Push the ball upfield along the wing, past the jockeying defender.

You don't need to beat the defender – just create enough space to hit a cross.

Quickly get your cross in before the defender has time to block the ball.

'CHECK-BACK' CROSS MOVE

A 'check-back' is when you stop the ball suddenly. Sprint down the wing as though you mean to cross with the foot nearest the touchline. Stop the ball, and drag it back downfield.

Your check-back will throw your marker. Hit a cross with your other foot, while he is off balance.

CROSSING DRILL

Place two markers as shown. Player A passes to player B, who dribbles along the wing. At the second marker, he crosses the ball to player C.

The players all move round one position, as shown, with player C taking the ball back to the first marker. The sequence then begins again.

★ Vary the position of player C to practise different lengths of cross.

★ Move the second marker for crosses nearer to, or further from, the goal-line.

★ Add a defender whose job is to prevent player B getting in his cross.

CROSSING MOVES

Scoring regularly from crosses takes more than just good technique on the part of the player crossing the ball. At least one team-mate in the penalty area has to find space to receive the ball and shoot. You can improve your chances of success by practising specific crossing moves.

RUNNING ONTO A CROSS

As you run in to receive a cross, make sure you stay onside. Don't get upfield of your team-mate with the ball, unless there are defenders between you and the goal.

As your team-mate crosses the ball, try to lose your marker (see page 4). Here, the striker runs as though to receive a long cross, then darts back to the near post area.

NEAR POST CROSSES

A cross to a player in the near post area gives him a good opportunity to head the ball down into the near side of the goal. If the goalkeeper is guarding the near post, the receiver can try glancing a header across into the far side of the goal.

To angle his header, the player flicks his head to the side as he makes contact with the ball.

USING A FLICK-ON HEADER

If you can't get a clear header at goal yourself, you may be able to flick the ball on to a team-mate who is in a better position to shoot.

For a flick-on header, use the top of your head, rather than your forehead, to make contact with the ball.

MID-GOAL MOVES

By varying the speed and height at which you deliver the ball, you can make crosses to the mid-goal area harder to defend against. In the example on the right, a low, hard cross into the mid-goal area allows a striker to use a side-on volley (see page 23).

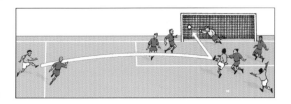

FAR POST MOVES

A goalkeeper will usually move over to cover crosses to the far post area. You may be able to wrong-foot him by heading the ball back across and into the other side of the goal, as shown in the picture below.

Because the goalkeeper is covering the far post, the striker coming in down the centre has a clear chance to score.

If you can see a team-mate running into a shooting position, you can head the ball down into his path, as shown on the right, rather than head it at goal yourself. This is known as laying the ball back.

USING AN INSWINGING CROSS

Here, the player on the left wing has used a check-back move (see page 17) to lose his marker. He then hits a cross with his right foot, making the ball swing in towards the goal.

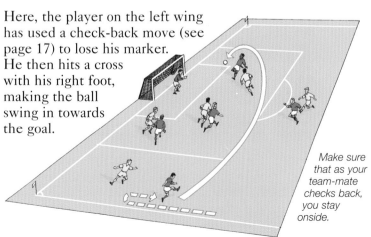

Make sure that as your team-mate checks back, you stay onside.

CROSSING LATE

One of the most effective cross moves is a cross hit almost on the goal-line. Swinging a late cross into the goalmouth gives your team-mates a chance to close right in on goal without being offside.

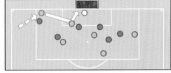

SOLO ATTACK

You don't always have to receive a through ball or a cross to find a chance to shoot. You may be able to try a solo attack on your opponents' goal, taking the ball past defenders yourself. A weaving run into the penalty area is a great way to put pressure on the other team's defence.

BASIC FEINTING

If you're dribbling towards goal with a defender straight in front of you, try to get past him by using a feint.

Feinting means fooling an opponent into thinking you are going to move one way, and then going the other.

The idea is to make the defender take his eye off the ball and watch your body instead, so you need to exaggerate your movements as much as possible.

Decide which side you're going to aim for. Pretend to go the other way, dropping your shoulder so that you look like you're about to swerve off in that direction.

As the defender moves across to cover you, quickly dodge past him in the opposite direction to your feint.

THE SCISSOR TRICK

Work on variations of the basic feint, so that you can use a range of feinting tricks to throw defenders off balance. Try using a check-back move, like the one on page 17, or use the 'scissor' feinting move shown here.

Here, the attacker makes as though to go left, but swings his foot over the ball.

He then uses his right foot to push the ball away quickly in the other direction.

As the defender follows the feint to the left, the attacker sprints past him.

TURNING ON THE EDGE OF THE PENALTY AREA

If you've received a pass on the edge of the penalty area from a team-mate downfield, you will have your back to the goal. To shoot, you need to turn to face the goal without losing the ball. As you receive it keep your body between the ball and your marker to 'shield' it. Then use one of the two turns below.

To turn to your non-kicking side, hook the inside of your foot around the ball. Lean across into your turn.

Drag the ball across your body and around to your side, turning as you do so on your non-kicking leg.

You can accelerate away past the defender, or hit an immediate shot past him to surprise the goalkeeper.

To turn to your kicking side, hook the outside of your foot around the ball. Lean into your turn.

Sweep the ball away to the side in an arc, turning your body to follow it so that you're facing the goal.

From an 'outside hook' like this, use your other foot to hit a fierce instep drive as you complete your turn.

TURN AND SHOOT DRILL

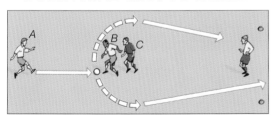

Try this drill with four players. Player A passes to B, who has to turn and shoot past defender C.

B scores one point for getting in a shot, and two for scoring. Have five goes, then change places.

STAR TURN

Being able to turn and shoot is a vital attacking skill. Here, George Weah (Milan) prepares to turn the ball away from defender Winston Bogarde (Ajax).

SHOOTING TECHNIQUES

You can use any of the basic kicking techniques to shoot, but the most effective choice will depend on whether the ball is rolling, bouncing, or in the air. You need to be able to strike the ball accurately and confidently, regardless of how you receive it.

THE INSTEP DRIVE SHOT

If you've dribbled into a shooting position, or received the ball along the ground, use your instep to drive a low, hard shot at goal.

Use your arms for balance.

Keep your head down, and your eye on the ball.

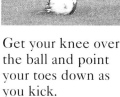

You need to get your non-kicking foot right up alongside the ball.

Get your knee over the ball and point your toes down as you kick.

Strike through the middle of the ball with your instep, keeping your head down. Follow through to power the ball away.

THE FRONT, OR FACE-ON VOLLEY

If you take the time to control the ball when it comes through the air, you may miss a chance to score. By hitting a shot 'on the volley' instead, you can often turn a half-chance into a spectacular goal. This is easiest when you are facing the ball.

Get yourself into position so that the ball will drop in front of you.

As the ball comes near, bring up your knee and point your toes.

Keep your head down and over your knee, so that your volley will stay low.

Strike the ball with your instep, stretching out your ankle as you kick.

THE SIDE-ON VOLLEY

To volley from the side, use this 'side-on' technique, also known as volleying on the half-turn. It is more difficult than a face-on volley, so watch the ball closely as it comes towards you in order to time it properly. Use your arms for balance.

Lean away from the ball, and swing your kicking leg up and around to your side.

Strike the ball with your instep. Hit it just above centre to keep your shot low.

Follow through by swinging your kicking leg right across your body.

SHOOTING ON THE HALF-VOLLEY

To half-volley, you kick the ball a split second after it bounces. It is quite hard to keep a half-volley shot down, as the ball is already starting to rise when you strike it.

Get your knee right over the ball as you kick, and keep your head down.

USING YOUR HEAD

From a high ball, such as a corner or cross, use a header to shoot. You have a better chance of scoring if you can direct the ball downwards. To do this, make contact with the top half of the ball. You may need to jump – if so, take off from one foot to gain maximum height.

Concentrate on the ball as you attack it.

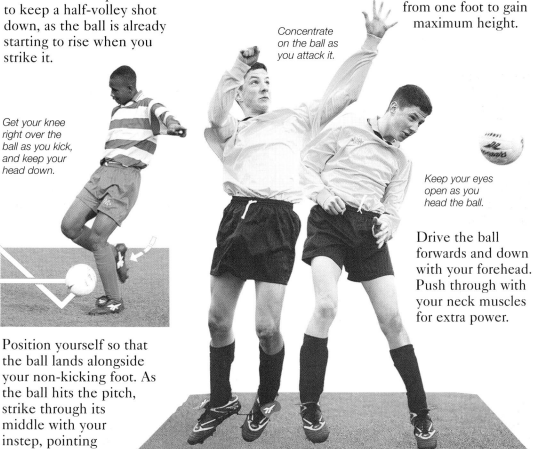

Keep your eyes open as you head the ball.

Drive the ball forwards and down with your forehead. Push through with your neck muscles for extra power.

Position yourself so that the ball lands alongside your non-kicking foot. As the ball hits the pitch, strike through its middle with your instep, pointing your toes down.

SHOOTING TACTICS

Shooting is about tactics as well as technique. Even a powerful shot won't go in if you hit the ball straight at the goalkeeper. To maximise your chance of scoring, you need to pick the most vulnerable part of the goal, and the best approach to beat the goalkeeper.

PICKING YOUR TARGET

Always try to keep your shot low. It's far harder for a goalkeeper to reach down from a standing position to cover a low shot than it is for him to stretch to reach a high one.

The further your shot is from the goalkeeper, the harder it will be for him to reach the ball. Aim just inside whichever post is furthest away from the goalkeeper.

Follow your shot in. If it rebounds from the goalkeeper, post or crossbar, you may get another chance to score.

Accuracy is more important than power – carefully pushing the ball past the goalkeeper is better than blasting it wildly at goal.

LONG RANGE SHOTS

Don't hesitate to shoot from a long way out because you're worried that your team-mates will blame you if you miss. The more shots you try, the more likely your team is to score. Bear in mind that players between you and the goal may block the goalkeeper's view, or even deflect your shot, making it harder to save.

A good striker shoots whenever he gets the chance. It's better to try for a goal and miss than not to try at all.

BEATING THE KEEPER

A goalkeeper will often try to reduce the area you can aim at by moving out towards you as you approach goal.

Here there are large areas on either side of the keeper to aim at.

By moving off his goal-line, the goalkeeper reduces the target areas.

If the goalkeeper 'narrows the angle' like this, and you think he is likely to block a shot to either side, try dribbling the ball past him instead.

1. You need to make the goalkeeper commit himself. Make as though to shoot past him so that he 'spreads' to block the ball.

2. Once he is on the ground, take the ball past him, or chip it over him. Run on and aim the ball carefully into the goal.

WHEN NOT TO SHOOT

However good your shooting skills are, you will sometimes find that your angle of approach and the defenders in your path mean that you've little chance of scoring. If you can see that one of your team-mates is in a better position, pass the ball to him.

ADVANCED SHOOTING

The mark of a good striker is the ability to create goals from half-chances. You need to be able to think quickly and have the determination to beat others to the ball. You also need to be inventive and go for unexpected shots.

OVERHEAD KICK

This acrobatic technique means you can shoot from a cross even if you have your back to goal. Don't try an overhead kick if other players are close to the ball, as you are likely to kick one of them.

Try to hit the top of the ball to aim your shot down.

Watch the ball as it approaches. Lift your non-kicking leg and lean back.

To reach the ball, take off from your kicking leg, lying back as you jump.

Whip your kicking leg up and over to strike the ball with your instep.

Put out your arms to break your fall. As you land, roll onto your shoulder.

DIVING HEADERS

To reach a low ball passing slightly ahead of you, a diving header may be your only shooting option. This is a shot that you must approach with courage and commitment.

Direct the ball by turning your head as you hit it.

Keep your eyes open as you head.

Launch yourself at the ball to give your header power.

Use your forehead to drive the ball forwards and down into the goalmouth.

Break your fall with your arms. Quickly get back into play.

SWERVE SHOTS

If your direct shooting line is blocked, you may be able to score by bending your shot. The secret of a 'swerve shot' is to strike the ball off-centre, making it spin.

If you hit the outside of the ball (the right-hand side if you use your right foot) with the inner part of your instep, your shot will swing away to your non-kicking side.

By hitting the inside of the ball (the left-hand side if you use your right foot) with the outside of your foot, you can make your shot swerve in the other direction.

ACUTE ANGLES

Don't be afraid to try a shot from an acute angle. It's harder to hit the target, but you may take the goalkeeper by surprise.

Here, the attacking player, approaching from an acute angle, drives a hard, low shot just inside the near post.

In this case, the attacker uses a bending shot to swing the ball around the keeper, so that it curls just inside the far post.

CHIPPING THE KEEPER

If the goalkeeper comes out as you approach the goal (see page 25), he leaves a space behind him. Try chipping the ball over his head, so that it drops down into the goal.

For a chip, kick the bottom of the ball with a sharp, stabbing action.

GETTING A TOUCH

You don't always need a clear shooting chance to score. You can often knock the ball into the goal simply by reacting quickly enough to get a touch on a cross or a deflection on a team-mate's shot.

Here, striker Hristo Stoichkov (Bulgaria) tries to get in a vital touch against Spanish goalkeeper Andoni Zubizarreta.

THROW-INS AND CORNERS

Whenever your team restarts play with a throw-in or corner kick, try to launch an immediate attack. The break in play gives you the chance to push upfield into good positions, and to use a rehearsed team move.

THROW-IN TIPS

The player nearest the ball when it goes out of play should take the throw quickly to catch defenders unprepared. His team-mates need to find or create space, so that there is at least one player in a good position to receive the throw.

Above: one blue player acts as a decoy to create space for his team-mate to receive the throw.

Right: the thrower gets straight back into the action, making a diagonal run upfield to receive a pass.

★ The thrower needs to deliver the ball so that the receiver can control it quickly and easily.

★ Whenever possible, the thrower should send the ball upfield, preferably to an unmarked team-mate.

★ Don't rush an attacking throw-in, or you're likely to do a foul throw, giving away possession of the ball.

USING A LONG THROW-IN

You can use a throw-in in the attacking third rather like a cross (see pages 16-19), with the added advantage that the player receiving the ball cannot be called offside. At least one player should perfect his long throw-in technique, so that he can reach the near side of the penalty area.

Because you can't be offside from a throw-in, you can all move right up, but usual offside rules apply once

the throw has been received. Here, the receiver uses a flick-on header to an onside team-mate.

ATTACKING FROM CORNER KICKS

The most direct way to attack from a corner kick is to cross the ball into the goal area, so that team-mates in front of the goalmouth can head or volley at goal. An inswinging cross to the near post area is the most popular option. The receiver can shoot, flick the ball on, or lay it back to a team-mate (see page 19).

Here, the yellow player at the near post flicks on a corner kick cross to a team-mate running in to shoot.

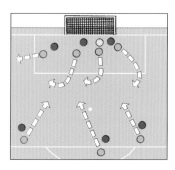

Attacking players in the centre have a number of options, as shown on the left. They can move out from the goal-line to find space as the cross comes in, or run in late from outside the penalty area.

You can use a far post cross, an outswinging cross or a driven cross (see page 19) to vary your corner kick tactics. Whichever you choose, your attacking players must work together to find or create space.

SHORT CORNER MOVES

By moving the ball out from the corner, you can create a different angle of attack. Instead of hitting a cross, the corner taker passes along the ground to a team-mate within easy range of goal. Three possible 'short corner' moves are shown below.

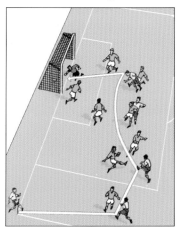

Here, two short passes move the ball from the corner to a player in a good position to hit a cross.

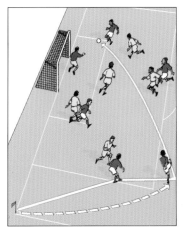

In this case, the corner kicker passes to a team-mate downfield, then overlaps him to receive a return ball.

Here, the attacker at the near post moves out along the goal-line to play a one-two with the corner taker.

FREE KICK ATTACKS

A free kick in the attacking third gives your team a great opportunity to attack. Because of the break in play, though, the other team has time to drop back and organize its defence. You need a well-thought-out, well-rehearsed move to find a weakness and score.

When a free kick is within range of your opponents' goal, some of their players will form a human wall to block your shot.

BEATING THE WALL

If the kick is direct, try swerving a shot around either side of the wall (see page 27), or chipping a shot over the top.

To take an indirect kick, you have to pass the ball. Try to create a good angle for a team-mate to shoot past the wall.

TIPS FOR TAKING FREE KICKS

A free kick shot is much more likely to go in if you can create an element of surprise to confuse the goalkeeper and defenders. Try using some of these free kick tips to fool your opponents.

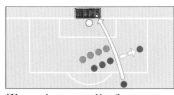

Try using a wall of your own players to hide your kick from the goalkeeper, so that he sees the ball as late as possible.

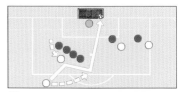

Use a dummy cross-over to disguise the direction of a free kick. Two attackers run in as though to kick, one from either side.

The first player to the ball dummies over it, leaving his team-mate to kick it in a different direction a split second later.

Use a more complicated indirect move to change the angle of attack. Don't be too ambitious – no more than three touches is best.

FREE KICKS FROM THE WING

If you get a free kick to one side of the penalty area, you probably won't be able to score with a direct shot because of the narrow angle. Use a cross instead.

In this picture, the kicker has hit an inswinging cross around the defensive wall to players running in down the centre.

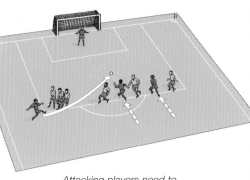

Attacking players need to time their run onto a cross to make sure they stay onside.

Instead of crossing directly from the kick, you can use a pass along the wing to move the ball further upfield first.

TAKING PENALTY KICKS

Of all restarts, a penalty offers the best chance of scoring a goal. If you can hit a low, hard, accurate instep drive, you're almost sure to beat the goalkeeper. As with all shots, you and your team-mates should follow in your penalty strike in case it rebounds.

Don't be hesitant – pick a target to aim for, and stick with your decision.

Try to look away from where you mean to kick, as this will help to fool the goalkeeper.

Important matches are sometimes decided by a penalty shoot-out between the teams, so don't neglect your penalty kick practice.

Roberto Baggio's penalty shoot-out miss put Italy out of the 1994 World Cup Final.

INDEX

If you would like to improve your soccer by attending a soccer course in your holidays, you can find out about different courses from:

Bobby Charlton International Ltd
Hopwood Hall, Rochdale Road
Middleton, Manchester M24 6XH
Tel: 0161 643 3113

First published in 1997 by Usborne Publishing Ltd, 83-85 Saffron Hill, London EC1N 8RT, England. Copyright © 1997 Usborne Publishing Ltd.

THE USBORNE SOCCER SCHOOL